D0496719

Please renew/return this item by the last date shown.

So that your telephone call is charged at local rate, please call the numbers as set out below:

	From Area codes 01923 or 020:	From the rest of Herts:
Renewals:	01923 471373	01438 737373
Enquiries:	01923 471333	01438 737333
Textphone:	01923 471599	01438 737599

L32   www.hertsdirect.org/librarycatalogue

For Lukasz, the explorer

www.dragonbloodpirates.co.uk

ORCHARD BOOKS
338 Euston Road, London NW1 3BH

First published in 2008 by Lothian Children's Books,
an imprint of Hachette Livre Australia
First published in the UK in 2010 by Orchard Books

ISBN 978 1 40830 740 3

Text © Dan Jerris 2008
Skull, crossbones and ragged parchment image © Brendon De Suza
Map illustrations on pages 4–5 © Rory Walker, 2008
Pull-out map designed by Kinart
All other illustrations © Orchard Books 2010

The right of Dan Jerris to be identified as the author of this work has been
asserted by him in accordance with the Copyright, Designs and Patents Act, 1988.

A CIP catalogue record for this book is available from the British Library.

10 9 8 7 6 5 4 3 2 1

Printed in Great Britain by J F Print Ltd., Sparkford

Orchard Books is a division of Hachette Children's Books,
an Hachette UK company.

www.hachette.co.uk

Dragon Blood Pirates

Idols and Ivory

Dan Jerris

ORCHARD BOOKS

Sabre Island

Town

Dragon's Stomach

Snake Island

Ghost Island.

Dragon Blood Islands

Pirate Mateys and Scallywags

Alleric (Al) Breas: Lives in Drake Drive and owns a mysterious sea trunk that takes him to the Dragon Blood Islands.

Jack Seabrook: Al's best friend.

Blacktooth McGee: A very nasty pirate who runs the brigantine *The Revenge*.

Flash Johnny: Blacktooth's devious and greedy cabin boy.

Snakeboot: A magical white three-legged cat with purple eyes. Legend has it he once belonged to a terrifying pirate called Vicious Victor.

Pigface McNurt: Blacktooth's bosun; a massive pirate with a ring through his nose.

Snotty Nell: A horrible one-eyed pirate who sails a frigate called *The Tormentor*.

Grenda: Snotty Nell's daughter.

Sharkbait: Snotty Nell's one-legged bosun.

Vampire Zu: Snotty Nell's huge first mate.

Gunner: The pirate captain of the ship *The Booty*.

Mozzy: *The Booty*'s bosun (petty officer).

Slicer: *The Booty*'s cook.

Mahoot: Captain Gunner's cabin boy.

Grandfather: Mahoot's grandfather and guardian of the swimming elephants on Sabre Island.

Stanley Spong: A crooked, sneaky trader who cheats people.

Vicious Victor: A pirate ghost. He used to pillage the Dragon Blood Islands and he stole Prince Alleric's magical sabre.

Prince Alleric: The prince who once ruled Sabre Island but disappeared in mysterious circumstances.

Halimeda (Hally) Breas: Al's younger sister.

Greeny Joe: A shark so big and old that mould grows on his skin, making him glow green in the dark.

Return to Pirate Land

Alleric Breas stood in front of a dusty mirror in the attic at number five Drake Drive. He adjusted his tricorn pirate hat and dusted his blue frockcoat. "Are you ready to go back and see if that treasure was real?" he asked his best friend, Jack, remembering all the jewels and gold they'd seen as they'd left Alleric Castle on their last adventure in the Dragon Blood Islands.

Jack Seabrook sat on the floor pulling

on his black buckled shoes. He stood, put his hand in the pocket of his burgundy coat, and pulled out a small ivory elephant. He inspected it for a second, took a deep breath and announced, "I'm ready. I want to see the elephants again, too!"

Beside the boys a three-legged white cat pawed at an old sea trunk.

Al saluted. "Let's go." He reached down and patted the cat. "Snakeboot's ready to go, too."

Just as the boys stepped towards the sea trunk the attic door burst open.

A girl with curly hair, shorts and a T-shirt stood at the door. "Are you playing pirates?" asked Al's sister, Hally.

"No," said Al, "we're just standing here dressed in pirate outfits."

"Can I be a pirate?"

"No!" said Al. "This is a boys' game."

"I want to play!" Hally whined.

"You can't," Al grouched, "so please leave." He gave his sister a push and shut the door.

Hally heaved the door open and stuck her head back into the room. She pointed at the cat. "Furgus doesn't need to play pirates," she said. "I want him."

"You can't have him," said Al, annoyed that his sister called the cat Furgus.

"Dad! screamed Hally. "Al won't let me play pirates and he won't let me have Furgus!"

Dad's voice floated up from downstairs. "Alleric Breas! If you won't let Hally play pirates you can at least let her have the cat."

"See?" said Hally. She poked her tongue out, pushed her way into the room and scooped the cat into her arms.

When she left, Al turned to his best friend. "Do you still want to go? Snakeboot's always come with us and showed us how to get back."

"Yep," said Jack, "but I reckon if we leave the door open, Snakeboot will follow us when Hally gets sick of playing with him."

"That's true – he's a real pirate cat," Al said as he opened the attic door a crack so the cat could come in later. Then he and Jack went to the sea trunk.

If you were a fly on the wall you would

have seen two boys, dressed as pirates, open and peer inside an old trunk.

Then you would have been blinded for a second, as if a flash of bright sunlight had been reflected from a mirror. By the time your sight returned, the boys would have completely vanished.

The Elephants' Graveyard

Al and Jack found themselves squashed behind a gold elephant's bottom. The strong scent of incense told them they were standing behind the idol in the Elephant Temple on Sabre Island.

Jack's eyes lit up with pleasure. "We're just where we wanted to be," he said. "This is the first time we've landed somewhere and we're not about to be eaten by a snake or a shark!"

"Is that you, Jack?" came a voice.
The boys looked around the back of the
elephant and into the temple. Mahoot, *The
Booty*'s cabin boy, was there with his frail
grandfather.

"Mahoot!" cried Jack happily.

"Hello," said Al politely.

The old man smiled at the boys.

"How did you get behind the idol?"
asked Mahoot. "We didn't see you come in.
Captain Gunner said you had vanished inside
Alleric Castle and he's been a bit worried."

"We found a secret room and got lost,"
said Al, only telling half the truth. "Then we
found ourselves here."

"Well, Gunner's sailed off to town for
a few days, so Grandfather and I said we'd
keep an eye out for you, and here you are!"

The boys joined Mahoot and his
grandfather in front of the golden elephant
idol. "Where's its eye?" asked Al, noticing

with some distress that the idol's one
remaining emerald eye was missing.

"Captain Gunner suggested that I hide it," replied Mahoot's grandfather, "in case somebody tries to steal it."

"Does the emerald really help the elephants?" asked Jack.

Mahoot's grandfather nodded. "Once, the magical emerald eyes kept watch for anyone who might hurt the elephants. If the idol sensed evil from a ship sailing towards the island, a great storm would magically erupt and drive it away."

"Wow," said Al. "So how did Snotty Nell manage to steal the other eye?"

"She came for the emerald eyes, and not to hunt the elephants," answered Mahoot's grandfather. "She'd come before, to hunt the elephants, but she was overwhelmed by the power of the eyes. When she learned about the legend and the wonderful emeralds, she decided to steal them. The elephants and I caught her in the temple, and we managed to drive her away. Sadly, she took off with one of the eyes. Now there is only one eye and one power left."

"What's that?" asked Al.

"It opens the doorway to the elephants' graveyard," explained Mahoot. "The door opens when magical words are spoken, right here on the steps of the temple."

"An elephants' graveyard! Wow!" said Jack. "What happens there?"

"When the elephants are old and dying, they come to the temple. Grandfather takes them to their ancestors. For hundreds of years the elephants have known when to come," Mahoot told the boys. "When Grandfather dies, I will be the keeper of the elephants." He looked at his grandfather. "But I hope that day never comes," he added.

"It comes to us all," said Mahoot's grandfather. "But we won't worry about such things now. Instead, I think we should

all go back to my house for
some tea."

Just as they were about
to leave the temple, loud
voices echoed from the
jungle. "Many men are
coming," said Mahoot's
grandfather, as the noise
came closer.

A louder voice
carried in the wind.
"The idol'ss
eye iss in the
temple."

"Hide!" Al cried,
recognising the voice.
But it was too late. A
red-coated pirate
and his fearsome
crew were heading
straight towards them.

The Power of the Idol

Captain Blacktooth marched into the temple with his cut-throat pirates.

"You should be dead!" yelled Flash, Captain Blacktooth's cabin boy. He drew his knife, then strutted angrily towards Al and Jack. "We left you on Snake Island to die. Perhaps I should finish the job."

"Leave them!" ordered Blacktooth. He studied the golden idol and his eyes widened in surprise. "Where'ss itss eye?"

He turned on Mahoot's grandfather. "Hass someone sstolen it already?"

The old man ignored the question.

"I ssaid, where iss it?" Blacktooth snarled.

Mahoot's grandfather lowered his head and closed his eyes. He folded his thin arms peacefully across his chest and refused to answer.

"You'll talk," Blacktooth threatened. He signalled to his first mate. "Pigface, make the old man talk."

Pigface and the pirates grabbed the boys and Mahoot's grandfather and pinioned their arms behind their backs. "Now, old man," said Pigface menacingly, "either you'll tell us what you've done with the emerald or we'll feed these fine boys to the sharks."

"The emerald's not here!" cried Al. "It's cursed and you know it. Something bad will happen to you if you take it."

"Shut up," ordered Blacktooth.

Flash poked the point of his knife into Al's chest. Another pirate slapped his hand over Al's mouth and twisted his arm.
Al struggled but the man was too strong.

"Leave the boys alone," Grandfather demanded. "He's right. The idol will destroy anyone who takes the emerald."

"Total load of bunkum," Blacktooth snorted. "It's a hunk of tin, painted gold. It can't hurt a thing."

"It hurt Snotty," said Jack, "so it can hurt you."

The pirates gasped as they remembered Snotty Nell's terrible fate. She had lost her own eye in the mouth of a shark, just after stealing the idol's emerald eye.

"I'll hurt you," growled Blacktooth.
He drew his sword and stepped threateningly towards Jack.

"I call on the idol to save us," cried Mahoot's grandfather. His voice echoed in

the temple. His words stopped Blacktooth.
The superstitious pirate sucked in his breath
and looked around. Nothing happened.

"Ahh-haa!" he cried. "I told you. You'll
pay for your idle threatss."

He loomed over
Jack once again.
"Help us now,
oh Great Golden
Elephant," called
the old man. His
voice reverberated
eerily around
the temple.

In answer, a
harrowing shriek
erupted from the
idol, making the
hairs on Al's neck
rise. The pirates'
eyes became

bigger, and their faces paled. They shifted their feet, preparing to run. The uncanny cry grew louder, as if all the ghouls from the cemetery were gathering in the temple. Pigface let out a massive howl of fear, bellowing in terror. But the cry from the idol was fiercer, scarier and more blood-curdling than anything imaginable. Al shivered.

"Run! Run for your lives!" cried Flash.

Terrified of the unearthly clamour coming from the elephant idol, the pirates took to their heels and ran.

The Apparition

As the petrified pirates disappeared into
the jungle, the dreadful scream from the idol
subsided into what sounded like a sob.
Al decided to investigate. As he tiptoed
carefully towards the idol, a familiar voice
called, "Help! Help!"

A girl wearing shorts and a T-shirt
appeared from behind the idol, clutching
Snakeboot tightly in her arms. Tears
trickled down her face. "Where are we?"

she blubbed when she saw Al.

Al rushed towards his sister and gave her
a hug. "You're safe," he reassured her. "It's
my sister," he called to Mahoot and his
grandfather. Then he turned to Hally, who

was squeezing the cat in
panic. "Let go of the cat
and come and meet
some friends,"
he said soothingly.
Grandfather
peered at the girl
closely. Then he
cried, "Princess
Halimeda! How can
you be here?"
Jack stared at him in
disbelief. "It's Halimeda,
all right. How did you
know that? And she's a
nerd, not a princess."

Mahoot's grandfather ignored Jack and went to Hally's side. "My dear," he said, "put some clothes on. You can't walk around in your unmentionables. You must cover your shoulders and legs. There are boys here."

Hally looked around in disbelief.

"We can explain it all," whispered Al, as Mahoot's grandfather rushed into a corner and returned with a long cotton cloth. He draped Hally in the worn garment, stood back, and sighed in embarrassed relief.

After several minutes Hally calmed down. Al and Jack took her to one side and explained about their other adventures. Still disbelieving, Hally told the boys her story.

She was playing with Snakeboot when he ran off. She had followed him to the attic, where he had jumped into the sea trunk. Hally had leant over to get him out. But in the blink of an eye she'd discovered she was somewhere strange. She'd picked up Snakeboot but, terribly afraid, she'd screamed and squeezed him. The cat howled in pain and she howled in terror.

The boys realised it had been those echoing screams that had saved them all from the pirates.

When Al, Jack and Hally finished talking, Mahoot's grandfather came over and took Hally's hand. "Come, Your Highness," he cooed. "I'm so glad you're home. You'll need some sweet tea to refresh you after your journey."

"She's not a princess," explained Al. "She's just my sister and she followed me here."

"Yes," said Grandfather, "of course, Prince Alleric. That is how it should be. Your sister followed you when you went off to fight the pirates. She went away, too, and now you have both returned. Good days are coming back to Sabre Island."

"Your names are the same as those other people," said Jack. "It's a very strange coincidence, don't you think?"

Al had to agree. Magical sabres and chests, secret treasures and more mysteries than he had ever imagined floated around in his mind. "I wonder if the first Prince Alleric was my grandfather..." he thought. "I only knew him for a short time, but Hally and I were named after him and his sister. What if Grandad went through time and couldn't get back, and something has made it possible for us to do so?"

Al was also wondering whether he and Jack would have time to sneak off to Alleric Castle to see if they could find the secret treasure room again. They might even find clues about the location of the magical Dragon Blood Sabre...

"Come now," said Mahoot's grandfather,

interrupting Al's thoughts, "we should take Princess Halimeda for tea and then we'll visit the elephants."

"Grandfather," Mahoot tried to explain, "Al and his sister are just kids. Prince Alleric and Princess Halimeda were grown-ups

when they left."

Mahoot's grandfather smiled knowingly. "Whatever you say, Mahoot," he replied. Then, patting Hally's shoulder, he said, "They've missed you, my dear. Elephants never forget people, and they have their own language. You are still talked about, even though you've been missing a long time."

Mahoot shook his head, rolled his eyes in exasperation and gave up. Hally, her eyes still bulging with disbelief, followed the old man and Mahoot out of the temple.

Kidnapped

A mother elephant trumpeted a welcome and came out of the jungle.

"Aren't they amazing!" Jack cried excitedly, as the mother elephant lumbered towards them. Her baby held her tail with its trunk, then left its mother's side to snuffle Al with interest. Another elephant followed, along with the rest of the herd. The gentle creatures bent their knees and lowered their trunks.

"Are you going to ride the elephants?" asked Mahoot's grandfather.

"If it's OK with you, I'd like to explore Alleric Castle first," Al replied.

"I'll come with you," said Jack.

"I want to ride the elephants!" said Hally excitedly.

"We'll ride and you can treasure-hunt," said Mahoot as he took Hally's hand and climbed onto an elephant's knees. Mahoot and Hally were encircled in a large leathery trunk and lifted onto the elephant's back. Hally's face lit with joy and she forgot her fears as she rode off with Mahoot through the jungle.

Meanwhile, Al, Jack and Snakeboot made their way to the deserted Alleric Castle. They entered the silent, gloomy rooms, searching for the secret door. They went from room to room but saw nothing recognisable.

They climbed stairs and went down others, they zig-zagged and searched, but still nothing was familiar. Hours went by and they grew tired. "Snakeboot showed us the way last time," said Al. "I didn't really concentrate when we ran after him."

Jack patted Snakeboot. "Can you find the treasure room for us again?" The cat responded by sitting in the dust and licking his paws.

"He's not going to help," said Al after a few minutes. "We'll have to try again on our own."

The boys hunted till nightfall but they could not find the room with the secret door. Finally, exhausted, they gave up. "Perhaps we dreamt it," said Jack. "It was probably a trick that played with our minds as we faded away and went home."

"Probably," said Al, feeling very disappointed. "I guess if Snakeboot wants us to find it again, he'll help us when the time is right. It won't stop us searching for the magical sabre, though."

"No, but for now it's getting late. We should get back," said Jack.

That night, Mahoot's grandfather lit the lamps and served dinner. The roast chicken wrapped in banana leaves, saffron rice and leafy salad made Al's mouth water. The boys ate the meal hungrily and were just finishing when the elephants began to trumpet loudly.

"The elephants are scared," cried Mahoot. "Blacktooth may have come back!"

"We have to help them," said Jack, as the sounds of gunfire made everyone leap to their feet.

The squeals of the distressed elephants led them to the beach. There, several pirates had trapped the animals inside a wooden corral. The pirates held flickering torches and spears and were firing their guns into the air to frighten them. The poor creatures circled frantically, trying to escape their tormentors.

The mother elephants pressed themselves against the fence, desperate to protect their babies. The pirates poked their spears viciously at them, determined to separate them from their calves. As one poor creature was beaten away from her baby, another elephant pushed forward and took the punishment. The babies cried in terror as the scent of blood rose into the air.

Al couldn't watch any longer. With a mighty yell of outrage, he leapt at a pirate who was jabbing one of the mother elephants and tore the spear away from him. Jack launched himself at the feet of another pirate, toppling him to the ground. Mahoot and his grandfather also struggled with the men, pulling spears from their hands. Then Snakeboot sank his claws into a pirate's neck, making him drop his musket and torch.

The sudden assault confused the other pirates, who dropped their torches in surprise, extinguishing the fire lights. In the dark, the boys disarmed a few more men, but their cries had alerted the rest of the crew to the scuffle.

More pirates ran towards them from

further down the beach. In the dark, the new arrivals couldn't recognise friend from foe, grabbing at the first person they found. The pirates moaned and screamed as they fell to the ground attacking each other.

In the middle of the fighting, Al ran to the corral and opened the gate. Some elephants managed to escape, but Al's attempt to free them only lasted a minute. A huge pirate holding a torch loomed over him. Seeing the corral gate open, the pirate threw his weight against it and slammed it shut. He reached out and grabbed Al with one gigantic hand and pinned him to the gate. In the flickering light of his torch the pirate leered at Al with sharply pointed teeth.

"Vampire Zu!" exclaimed Al.

"The diamond stealer!" Vampire Zu bawled, dragging Al to his feet. As he glanced around, Al saw that Jack, Mahoot and his grandfather had also been captured.

Snotty Nell came over and inspected her prisoners. "You!" she snarled when she saw Al. "You rotten little diamond–stealing barnacle. You won't escape again." She pushed Al with the butt of her spear. "Tie them up," she ordered. "Do it extra tight."

Al struggled with all his might against the pirates, but they forced his hands and feet together and bound him tightly. Realising all was lost, he called out to Snotty Nell. "Captain Nell," he begged, "please leave the elephants alone."

Jack pleaded with her, too. "You're a mother, how can you take a baby away from its mother?"

"They're elephants," she growled, but despite her harsh voice Al thought she looked unsettled. She wiped a drool of mucus from her nose, glanced at the elephants for a second, and snorted dismissively. Turning back to Jack, she

snarled, "I don't want to hear your
voices again."

"I'll put a gag on them," said Sharkbait,
Snotty's one-legged bosun. "These boys are
full of tricks."

It didn't take long for the pirates to
separate the mother elephants from their
babies. They herded five baby elephants
down the beach and pushed them onto
large rafts. As the pirates rowed them away

towards *The Tormentor*, the mother elephants rammed themselves against the wooden corral. Frantically they managed to smash the walls and, trumpeting in panic, they waded into the water after their babies.

Afraid, Hally had been hiding in the jungle. When the pirates left, she ran out of her hiding place, her eyes full of fear. She undid the ropes binding Mahoot's grandfather and the boys. In a flash, Mahoot

raced along the beach. Under a tree was a small dinghy. "Help me!" he cried.

Al and Jack helped their friend pull the dinghy into the sea. They climbed in and Mahoot rowed with all his strength towards the mother elephants, who were swimming further and further out towards the pirate ship, anchored far offshore.

Within minutes, the boys came up beside one of the mother elephants. The poor creature was sobbing in distress as she swam. Mahoot jumped from the dinghy onto the animal's back. He leant forward, patted the elephant's head and lifted her huge ear. He softened his voice and, in a strange language of grunts and groans, he spoke to her. The elephant lifted her trunk. The boys listened in awe as the creature spoke back. As they watched, the elephants began communicating with each other. After a series of grunts, the mothers stopped

swimming, turned and headed back towards
the island.

Al and Jack took over the oars of the
dinghy and rowed beside the poor creatures.
"What did you say to them, Mahoot?"
asked Jack.

"I told them they would drown if they
kept swimming, as the pirates were sailing
far, far away," Mahoot explained. "I said we
would save their babies and bring them
home. The elephants trust us."

"We will bring their babies back,"
declared Jack. "Tell them we promise."

The Rescue

The Booty's sails appeared on the horizon the next day. When Captain Gunner dropped anchor he found four young people waiting anxiously for him. His eyes opened wide at the sight of Hally, but they quickly narrowed when he heard about the baby elephants' fate. "That Snotty's a vicious vagabond," he said. "Just for once, I'm gunner get my own back on her."

"So, can we rescue the elephants?" asked Jack.

"We will sail straightaway," replied Captain Gunner. "Hoist the mainsail," he called to Mozzy, the bosun, and the crew set to work.

The Booty was sailing towards town in under an hour. "Snotty got a big head start," said Al. "Will she have sold the babies already?"

"No," said Slicer, the cook. "Everything is sold on market day and that isn't until Wednesday. We have two days to find them."

When *The Booty* docked at nightfall, the crew disembarked and scattered throughout the town, searching for the elephants. Al, Jack, Mahoot and Hally followed Snakeboot as he bounded from the ship and ran off down the main street.

Snakeboot led them down a darkened alley, where he stopped outside a shop. "It's Spong's place," whispered Al, recognising the junk shop immediately. "Why has Snakeboot brought us here?" The cat answered by hiding behind some large boxes in the street. Following Snakeboot, the children crouched down out of sight, watching Stanley Spong's doorway.

Hally had fallen asleep on Al's shoulder, and Jack's head was nodding when a lantern light cut into the darkness further down the street. Snotty Nell and her daughter, Grenda, appeared, and walked towards

them. Al ducked his head out of sight
and elbowed Jack.

"Mum," they heard Grenda say. "I don't
want to go inside. The shop stinks and
Stanley spits everywhere."

Snotty Nell grabbed her daughter's
hand and pulled her along the street. "I'll
only be ten minutes," she said. "Spong has
a ringmaster he wants me to meet. He's
promised me a good price on the elephants."

Grenda kicked a rock on the road in
complaint, but followed her mother into
the shop.

Al and Jack crept up to the window
and peered in.

Snotty, Stanley Spong and a big fat man
with long greasy hair sat at a table. Grenda
fingered the merchandise that lay stacked on
a shelf at the back of the room. She picked
up a glass jar. It slipped from her fingers and
smashed onto the floor.

"Get her out of here!" Stanley Spong yelled angrily. Then he spat into a brass bowl on a bench. "Get her out before she breaks something valuable."

Snotty pointed to the door and Grenda almost skipped to it with joy. "Stay just outside," warned Snotty. "I don't want you getting lost."

"I promise to stand right on the welcome mat," answered Grenda.

The boys ducked back to their hiding place. Hally was still blissfully asleep, her head resting on an old box. "What should we do now?" whispered Mahoot. "Will we wait and follow them?"

"They'll probably just go back to their ship," Al whispered back, "and I'm guessing the elephants aren't there."

"We could ask Grenda," suggested Jack. "She might tell us." He didn't wait for anyone to agree before he picked up a

pebble and lobbed it at Grenda. The stone
hit her skirt. She looked around.

"*Pssst*," hissed Jack.

Grenda looked around in surprise.

"*Psst*, Grenda," Jack called. "Come here."

Grenda took a step towards the boxes.

"Who's there?" she whispered.

"Me, Jack." He stood up and beckoned his old acquaintance. Grenda made a tentative move and Jack crept over to her in the middle of the road.

"If Mum sees you and me talking," hissed Grenda, "I'll be locked in the galley for days."

"I'll be quick," said Jack. "Did you know your mum has taken some baby elephants?"

"Yep," said Grenda. "She's selling them. Probably tomorrow. That's why we're here."

"Where are they?" asked Jack.

"Why would I tell you?" said Grenda.

"Because," whispered Jack, thinking quickly, "if you do, I'll give you a present."

"I've got to see it first," she said.

Jack put his hand in his pocket and pulled out the ivory elephant carving he had been carrying around. "It's real ivory," he told her.

"It's very small," she said, holding her hand out for it.

Jack handed the carving to Grenda, and she put it in her pocket. "It's mine now, and I'm *not* going to tell you where the elephants are!" With those words she turned her back on Jack and returned to Stanley's doorway. Jack went back to the pile of boxes.

"Great," said Al. "That was just great. Now Grenda knows we're here and she'll tell her mother, who will double guard the elephants. We're worse off than before!"

"Maybe Grenda won't tell," argued Mahoot. "She can be mean sometimes, but she's not dreadful."

Several minutes went by, then Snotty Nell appeared. She took Grenda's hand and headed down the street.

"What now?" said Mahoot.

"We follow them, since there's nothing else to do," Al answered, shaking Hally awake.

Snotty Nell and her daughter walked back towards the docks. Once or twice Grenda looked behind her and gave her followers a little wave. Then, just before Snotty turned onto the main street, Grenda suddenly flung her arm out to the right-hand side of the street and pointed down an alley. "See?" said Jack. "She's not all bad."

"I hope this isn't a trick," said Mahoot.

The children and Snakeboot turned to the right and walked along the alley. It led them out of town and down a winding country road. Onwards they went in the moonlight, often stumbling over bumps and corrugations in the road. "She's fooled us," said Mahoot after a while.

"Probably getting us back for sending her down the wrong path in the tunnels on Death Island," agreed Al. "I wouldn't—" His words were cut short as the sound of a crying elephant reached their ears.

They hurried forward and came to a stone storehouse. The door was barred. Just inside

the bars, sound asleep on the ground, was
Vampire Zu.

"What can we do to get them out?"
whispered Jack. His voice carried to the
sharp-hearing elephants trapped inside, who
began to trumpet hopefully.

Vampire Zu lifted his head. "Quit
your bellyaching!" he roared angrily at
the creatures. "Enjoy your last night on
holiday!" He chuckled, rolled over and went
back to sleep.

An hour later, at nearly midnight, the
children returned to *The Booty*. They told
Captain Gunner how they'd found the
elephants and about Vampire Zu sleeping
behind the locked and barred door.

"We have to get him to leave somehow,"
said Jack.

"We could try to lure him out,"
suggested Hally.

"How would we do that?" asked Gunner. "He's not gunner move. He's under orders."

"Orders from Snotty Nell," said Al excitedly. "One of you could dress up as Snotty and call him out. Hally could dress up as Grenda and he'd be fooled in no time. Then when he comes out, we could overpower him."

"Who's roughly Snotty's size?" asked Jack, looking at the pirates.

The crew immediately straightened up. "None of us are as short as she is," said Slicer. "And we're not dressing up as a girl."

"It's dark," Al told them. "From a distance he'd just see a person in a dress and a little girl. We could fool him." Al looked at Mozzy, the slightly built bosun. "You'd be the right size."

"It's a good idea," agreed Hally. She reached out and held Mozzy's hand. "I'm brave enough if you are," she said.

Her challenge was too much for Mozzy;
he couldn't refuse. "No one's allowed to
tease me, though," he grouched.

The plan in place, just before dawn, Gunner
and his pirate crew were hiding down the
road from the storehouse. Mozzy, holding
Hally's hand, limped up the road towards the

door. "Vampire!" he called in a high voice. "Help! I've twisted my ankle." He fell to his knees. "Ewwwww!" he wailed, then he wiped his nose with the back of his hand.

"Come and help Mum!" Hally cried.

Vampire stared down the road.

"Help her now!" yelled Hally. "Her leg is all twisted!"

Vampire jumped to the order. He made his way towards Mozzy and Hally. He hadn't gone very far when Gunner and four of his crew jumped out at him. Big as Vampire was, he was no match for five men. They leapt upon him, forced him to the ground and tied him up.

They'd done it! Within minutes the five baby elephants were running along the road with Gunner and his pirate crew. "Wait till Snotty hears about this," crowed Gunner.

The Eye
of the Idol

Gunner anchored *The Booty* just off the
beach where the baby elephants had been
kidnapped. His crew rigged strong ropes from
the mast and the main yardarm, and with a
winch, the pirates lowered the baby elephants
into the water. Mahoot put his hands to his
mouth and made a long, high-pitched call. An
answering trumpet came from the jungle and
within minutes the grown-up elephants had
arrived on the beach. Already in the water,

the babies swam for their lives towards their family, crying loudly. The mothers, hearing their little ones, swam out to meet them.

Once all the elephants were ashore the mothers circled and sniffed their babies, checking that no harm had come to them. Then they wrapped their trunks around the little ones and turned towards Gunner's pirate ship. The herd stood nervously, but seeing Mahoot, Al and Jack, they bent their giant knees and bowed low to the crew. Then they turned and walked back into the jungle.

"That's a good deed done," said Gunner, wiping a sentimental tear from his eye. Then, not wanting to be seen as a softy, he turned to Mozzy. "Look alive! We have some treasure hunting to do. We're gunner set sail now in search of plunder. We've wasted enough time."

"Would you mind if we stayed here for

a few days?" asked Jack. "We'd like to stay with the elephants."

"And Grandfather," added Mahoot. "I've barely seen him."

"Yes," said Al, "And I really want to look around Alleric Castle and see if there are any clues to finding the sabre!"

Gunner scratched his head for a few minutes and thought. "Well, I'm not happy about leaving you here, but you boys have been lucky. Even that sister of yours hasn't given me any trouble." He smiled at Hally. "How about I give you two days? Then we'll be back. I expect if anyone's gunner find something it'll be you lot."

"Thanks," said Al.

Gunner prepared to depart. "Lower the ship," he ordered. "We're leaving a treasure-hunting party behind."

As the children, with Hally clutching Snakeboot, were lowered into the water, Gunner called out, "Hally, I'll get you some sea clothes. You can't go around in that old cloth with your underpants showing!"

Hally and the boys soon arrived at Mahoot's grandfather's house. "He will be so pleased we saved the elephants," said Mahoot as he opened the door. "Hello!" he called, but there was no reply.

"He's probably in the temple," suggested Jack. The children set off to find him.

They hadn't gone far when they saw Mahoot's grandfather, gagged and bound to a tree. His bald head was bowed in sorrow. "Grandfather!" the children cried, racing to help him.

"What happened?" asked Mahoot angrily as he undid the ropes, rubbing his grandfather's wrists to get his circulation moving.

Mahoot's grandfather struggled to his feet, stumbling as he tried to walk. "We must hurry," he said. "Blacktooth has the eye of the golden elephant!"

"How did he get it?" asked Al.

"He captured me," explained Mahoot's grandfather. "His men were carrying blunderbusses and he threatened to kill all the elephants unless I told him where the eye

was hidden. I knew he meant it, so
I had to tell him."

"Has he taken the emerald to his ship?"
asked Al.

"No," said the old man, "he's hoping
to open the secret door to the elephants'
graveyard. He wants the ivory from
there, too."

"We have to stop him," said Jack,
and he began to run
towards the temple.
"Wait!" Al shouted.
"We need to have a
plan. We have to
think of a way to get
the emerald back."
"Is it easy to open the
door to the graveyard?"
asked Hally.
"No," said Mahoot's
grandfather, "the

secret words are written on the altar. Blacktooth doesn't know how to say them yet. He was going to take me with him, but he was afraid I'd summon the ghosts again, so his pirates tied me up. I'm so lucky you found me."

"If he works out the secret words and ends up with the ivory and the emerald, he'll be back for more," said Jack, "and he won't worry about killing the elephants then."

"Is there a way we can spy on them and see what they're doing?" Al asked Mahoot's grandfather.

"There's a hidden doorway," he replied. "Follow me."

Carefully they approached the temple. Mahoot's grandfather sneaked around the back and showed them a doorway covered in vines. They pulled the leaves to one side and peered into the temple. The golden elephant idol was so close they could almost touch it and just in front of the statue were

Blacktooth and his pirates. Holding the
magical emerald in his hand, Blacktooth
reached up and put it in the idol's empty
eye socket. The stone glowed with
mysterious power and its light shimmered
through the shadows of the temple.

Blacktooth bent forward and studied some
words on the base of the altar:

AZGDPR NAROEI
APEONT
NTARNA IATOA

"Asshgdarprr naroooeii," Blacktooth
stumbled. He tried again several times.
Spit flew out of his mouth, but nothing
happened. "Flaming rubbish!" he shouted
angrily. He grabbed Flash by the coat. "You
learnt to read in school, didn't you?"

"I went to grade three," said Flash. "The kids there were all stupid, so I left."

"Well, that's better than me," said Blacktooth. "You do it."

Flash tried to read but his tongue faltered over the strange words. "The star things don't help," he said. "They didn't teach star letters at my stupid school."

"Pigface, you have a go," ordered Blacktooth.

"I think that's French," said Pigface. "I can't speak French."

Al had seen enough; he had thought of a plan. Tapping his friends on the shoulders, he beckoned them away. When they were out of the pirates' hearing, Al said, "Hally, do you think you can take Snakeboot and sneak around the back of the idol to where you spooked Blacktooth last time?"

"I can try," she said bravely, "but I'm really scared. What if they catch me?"

"I'll come with you," said Jack. "We can do it together." He looked at Al. "Are we going to scream and frighten them again?"

"Yes," said Al, "but only when I give you the signal."

"Can you howl like you did when Hally squeezed you, without one of us pulling your tail?" Jack asked their white-haired friend.

Snakeboot purred in answer and Jack was sure the cat gave him a smile. "You're such a cool dude."

"What are you planning to do?" Mahoot asked Al. "Their screams won't be enough to scare the pirates away this time."

"You and your grandfather and I are going to ask the elephants to help us," Al replied. "Jack and Hally, try to get behind the elephant idol. When you hear me whistle, that will be the sign to make all the noise you can."

Fifteen minutes later, Jack, Hally and Snakeboot were hiding behind the elephant idol. Their movements had gone unnoticed because the pirates were bent over the front of the altar, studying the secret words and arguing about how to say them.

A loud whistle gave the signal. Snakeboot lifted his head and caterwauled. Jack shrieked like a madman and Hally wailed like a

banshee. The ear-splitting noise reverberated out into the temple, shaking the air and terrorising the pirates.

At the same time Al, Mahoot and Grandfather rode into the temple on the backs of three large bull elephants. Four more angry elephants followed behind to join the battle.

Seeing their hated enemies, the elephants

rolled their eyes in rage, trumpeted and charged. The first bull elephant hooked his long tusks under a pirate and threw him into the air. Another pirate was tossed high and fell heavily into a corner. The rest of the pirates panicked and ran. Blacktooth made a grab for the eye of the idol, but Al was too quick for him. The boy leant down from the elephant he was riding and grabbed the emerald eye before Blacktooth could snatch it away.

Then, almost simultaneously, another massive elephant charged towards Blacktooth. Before the pirate captain could be tossed like a basketball, he ran for all he was worth.

Soon the temple was empty of pirates, the last of them having run, bloodied and bruised, into the jungle. Al, Mahoot and his grandfather climbed down from the elephants' backs and joined Jack, Hally and Snakeboot.

"Now," said Al, " We need to call all the elephants. We have to hide somewhere because Blacktooth will come back and he'll be seething. If he can't get the emerald he'll want revenge."

Mahoot and his grandfather spoke to the brave elephants. The giant beasts lifted their trunks, called out and within minutes all the elephants had gathered outside the temple.

"There is only one safe place," said Mahoot's grandfather, "and that is in the elephants' graveyard."

Al admired the glittering emerald for just a moment before putting it back into the elephant idol's eye. Mahoot's grandfather raised his voice, his magic words ringing through the temple. As he spoke, Al read the words on the altar. He realised they were in code – he had seen something like this before.

At the same time a loud grinding of rock

on rock alerted them all to the movement of the idol. Slowly the golden elephant swung to one side and a massive doorway opened in the back of the temple.

One by one, all the elephants walked through. When the last elephant was safely inside, Mahoot's grandfather reached up and removed the eye of the idol. Then he, Mahoot, Jack, Al and Hally entered the elephants' graveyard and the secret door shut behind them.

It was pitch dark. Grandfather lit a torch that was just behind the door. He collected more torches and handed them to everyone.

All around them lay the bones of hundreds of elephants, glowing white in the flickering light. Great ribs and rounded ivory tusks hung with spiderwebs.

The elephants stamped nervously in the confined space, but they stayed quiet. The great beasts understood that their lives depended on their silence.

The cave would have been frightening, but a gentle wind wafted through the air with a sweet scent from the jungle. One by one, the elephants moved around the graveyard and touched the massive skeletons of their ancestors with their trunks. "It's as if they're greeting them," whispered Jack.

"They are," said Mahoot's grandfather. "They remember their ancestors. They are paying their respects."

No one could tell day from night, so when they grew tired they made themselves comfortable between the legs of the elephants and fell asleep. Grandfather stood guard and lit more torches. When they woke up he told them stories about the Dragon Blood Islands.

The one Al liked the most was the story about two dragons – a good dragon and a bad dragon – who fought each other over some jewels. They flew into the sky and cut each other with their claws. Their blood dripped down into the ocean, boiled and frothed and then became solid. This was how the Dragon Blood Islands came to be. Some islands were peaceful and beautiful,

like Sabre Island,
but others were
dangerous and
frightening.

After Mahoot's
grandfather had
told all of his
wonderful
stories, they
sat quietly
and patted the
elephants.

"Can we go yet?" Jack
asked after what seemed like days and days.

"We've got to stay here till we think
Blacktooth has gone and Captain Gunner
has returned," said Al. "Blacktooth could be
hunting the island for us. We've only slept
once. I think we should sleep at least twice."

Hally's stomach rumbled. "I'm really
hungry," she complained.

"We can be hungry for a day," Jack reassured her. "Being hungry is better than being captured by Blacktooth and risking the elephants' lives."

Hally nodded and didn't complain again.

Not one elephant made a noise. The hours went by slowly. So slowly, in fact, that Al watched a spider build an entire web between a dead elephant's ribs. Grandfather extinguished the torches and, once again, they all slept with the elephants.

When they awoke, Mahoot asked, "Can we risk going out now?"

"I think so," said his grandfather. "The elephants must eat and so must we." He held the emerald high, spoke the magical words and the door opened.

The sun shone brightly as they emerged, but there were no pirates in sight.

Treasure Map

When they came out of the temple,
Grandfather took them to his house and
they devoured some food. Afterwards,
Mahoot and his grandfather decided they
should take the elephants deep into the
jungle for protection.

Al, however, wanted to explore Alleric
Castle while they waited for Captain Gunner
to return. "Come on, Hally," he said. "You
haven't seen it. We might find some treasure."

Hally's eyes lit up at the word 'treasure'.

Once again Al stepped through the broken doors of Alleric Castle. Jack showed Hally the fine picture of Prince Alleric hanging in the foyer, pointing out the magical sabre that could make the prince fly through time and space to gather treasure.

They wandered down a long hallway and up some stairs to the second floor. In one room Hally found the broken statue of a woman. The head had been knocked off and lay on the floor. "How sad," said Hally. She picked up the head and placed it on the body of the statue. The piece fitted perfectly. "It almost looks new now," she remarked.

Al's eyes were taken by the inscription under the statue:

TEE⭐DRE HAIDER
E⭐SS⭐E SE➝☆
TUHN⭐S⭐ RRIPH

Under the inscription was a carving of a
sabre. Having heard Mahoot's grandfather
say the other magic words earlier, Al realised
this message could be decoded in the same
way. He bent down and quickly wrote
something in the dust on the floor with his
finger. Then he reached out and put his
thumb on the sabre. There was a sudden
loud click as a small drawer popped
out of the base.

The children peered into the drawer.
"A diamond ring!" cried Hally. She picked
up the ring and put it on her little finger.
It fitted perfectly.

"And some writing paper," added Jack.
He held up a parchment. "A map!"

"I hope that map's gunner be for me," said
a voice from behind them.

The children turned to see their friend.
"Captain Gunner!" they cried joyfully. "We
think we've found a treasure map!"

Gunner took the map and studied it
carefully.

"Can you recognise the island on the
map?" asked Al.

"Unfortunately I can," the pirate replied.
"It's Cannibal Island." He shivered in dread.
"And it's the same island where Blacktooth
has his fort."

"Will we go looking for it?" asked Jack.

With a worried expression, Captain

Gunner bit his lip. He gave the children an odd look and said, "I wouldn't usually, but you kids have been lucky. I'll risk it." He held out the map. "Look for yourselves, though. Most of the map is missing. We'd be walking blind and we'd have to dodge the cannibals. Are you up for it?"

"Not me," said Hally. "I'll stay here with Mahoot's grandfather."

"We are!" said the boys in unison.

"You, the cat and the old man can stay," Captain Gunner told Hally. "We've got to re-provision with fresh water but we shall sail on the next tide."

Home

While the ship was being provisioned,
Mahoot returned from the jungle. Gunner
gave the boys some buckets. "Off you go
and earn your keep," he ordered.

Jack looked up at the hot sun. "Ohhhh,"
he complained.

"Everyone's equal on a pirate ship. Cabin
boys have to work hardest, though," Gunner
responded. Then he beckoned Hally. "I like
that ring on your finger," he said.

"Do you want it?" asked Hally, expecting the pirate to take it from her.

"Goodness, no," replied Gunner, "but while I was away I got you something to go with it." He walked to a locker, bent and picked up a parcel. He handed it to Hally.

Hally opened it and inside she found a fine blue dress with puffed sleeves and a skirt that reached the ground. "I think it should be your size," said Gunner.

Hally thanked him, then went below deck and put the dress on. It fitted perfectly. She ran off to join the boys, who were slaving in the hot sun, carrying buckets of water.

A hogshead barrel half-filled with water was stored down in the galley. The boys had to go to a creek, fill two buckets each and struggle back down the track. Then they had to fill a small barrel of water in the lifeship. When that barrel was full, Slicer rowed back

to *The Booty* and hauled it aboard. There it
was emptied into the hogshead in the galley.
It took sixteen full buckets of water to fill
each small barrel on the lifeship, and the
boys had to fill eight barrels.

Sweat was running down their backs,
and they had only made
one trip, when Hally
joined them. She ran
towards her brother
as he bent to fill his
buckets in the
creek. "Look, I
have a funny
dress like
Grenda," she
said, and to show
off the dress she
did a spin. The
skirt flared.

"My back

hurts," groaned Jack, ignoring her.

Snakeboot came up to her and pawed at her dress. "Furgus likes it," said Hally.

Al also ignored her as he hoisted his buckets and carried them down the track.

"Fine," grouched Hally. "I hate it here anyway." She flounced off and sat on a rock. "I wish I was home!" she shouted.

Snakeboot jumped into her lap and rubbed his head against her arms. Then he leapt off and ran into the jungle. Hally followed. The cat went into a small, overgrown gazebo, which once must have been a place where people rested on a fine afternoon near the bubbling creek. Now, covered with vines, it was nearly invisible. Hally followed Snakeboot inside and climbed up the stairs. At the top there was a small room with a door. Pushing the door open, she stepped inside...

"Where's Hally?" Al asked when he came

back up the path to the creek with empty buckets.

"Don't know," said Jack. "I saw her follow Snakeboot down that path."

"I hope she isn't lost," said Al. "We'd better look for her."

When Al and Jack searched the jungle, they too found the vine-covered gazebo and, soon after, the small room with the door. As they entered the room a familiar tingling in Al's hands and feet told him he was going home.

Seconds later, he found himself back in his attic. Jack soon appeared beside him; Hally and Snakeboot were already there. Hally had taken off her new dress and was hanging it on an old coathanger near the mirror. "I'd better put the ring somewhere safe," she said. "I don't think Dad would understand how I got it."

The boys agreed.

"That was amazing," said Jack after he had changed out of his sea-going pirate clothes. "I feel really proud that we saved the baby elephants."

"It was exciting," agreed Hally. "But I don't like pirates, not at all. I did like being a princess, though."

"Jack, your mother's on the phone!" Al's Dad's voice came to them from downstairs. "She wants you home to do your chores."

"Coming!" called Jack. He smiled at his friends. "Chores are dead easy. Make a bed, suck a bit of dirt up with a vacuum cleaner, stack the dishwasher."

"Yes, nothing like the chores in the Dragon Blood Islands," said Al. No electricity or running water means that even having a bath is really hard work!"

"Cleaning the toilet has to be the worst!" Jack added.

"Pirates have no toilet paper," whispered Hally, her face reddening.

"And no flush!" exclaimed Jack. "And no soap."

"I don't like cleaning the toilet at home, but back there..." Al held his nose.

"Why do pirates call the toilet 'the head'?" asked Hally.

"I've no idea," replied Jack.

Al laughed. "I vote Hally asks Captain Gunner when we go back!"

"No way," said Hally. "I'm going downstairs to empty the dishwasher." And with those words she flounced out of the room.

"Sounds good to me," said Jack. "I'd better get home to earn my pocket money."

"And I'm going to help Dad bring in the washing," said Al. "Easy!"

Clues to the Puzzles

To decode the cryptic messages on pages 68
and 82, draw a grid that's five columns
across and six rows down. Write each
word downwards in a column, starting a
new column for each word. Put the stars in
the same square as the letters before them,
not in a separate square. You can then read
the message across the grid. (A star denotes
the end of a word in the message.)
If you need help decoding these messages,
visit www.dragonbloodpirates.co.uk

Arrr! Ahoy there, mateys!

hoist the sails and drop the anchor:
ye have some treasure to find!

One swashbucklin' reader will win a haul of booty, including an Xbox console and games and an iTunes voucher, and twelve runners up will win a Dragon Blood Pirates booty bag.

For a chance to win, ye must dare to unearth the treasure using the Dragon Blood Islands map from *Death Diamond* (also available to download at www.dragonbloodpirates.co.uk), and the six big pirate stickers that are inserted in every book.

Each of the six Dragon Blood Pirates books contains a clue revealing an island protected by a dastardly pirate, and a sticker of the pirate to place on your map. When ye have solved the six clues, and have placed the six stickers, there will remain only one island, where the pirate booty be.

To win, enter online at
www.dragonbloodpirates.co.uk

Or send your name, address and the name of the island where the treasure lies to:

Dragon Blood Pirates Treasure Hunt
338 Euston Road, London NW1 3BH

Best o' luck, me hearties!

To find where the pirate sticker
from *Idols and Ivory* should go,
ye must find the answer to
the clue that lies below:

**This fearsome pirate protects
with all his might,
The Dragon Blood Island
with cliffs that are white.**

If you get stuck, fear not, for there be
extra clues hidden on
www.dragonbloodpirates.co.uk
To uncover them ye must enter a password,
that be the answer to the following question:

*What be the name of Jack and Al's
three-legged cat?*

Sabre Island

Snakeboot, the three-legged white cat, sat purring happily on an old sea trunk in the attic of Alleric Breas's house at number five Drake Drive. Al and his best friend, Jack, were also in the attic.

"Hally's playing next door," said Al. "It might be a good time to go back to Sabre Island."

"I know it sounds mean, but it would be good to go back on our own," said

Jack. "Captain Gunner's ship, *The Booty*, might still be there. And I really want to go hunting for treasure!"

"It's not really being mean," said Al. "Hally didn't want to go to sea again, anyway. She said she was too scared to go to Cannibal Island. I don't think she'll mind if we go on our own."

"Do you think we could get back to exactly the same time and place as when we left?" Jack asked his friend.

Snakeboot arched his back, jumped down from the sea trunk and clawed at the lock on the front of the trunk.

"I think Snakeboot is saying yes," Al replied. "And I can't wait to see if that treasure map we found in Alleric Castle really leads us to jewels and gold."

"Let's get dressed, then." Jack reached up and pulled down two sets of pirate clothes from a shelf.

The boys quickly changed clothes. Al
grabbed an old iron key and unlocked the
sea trunk. He lifted the lid and Snakeboot
leapt inside. The boys stepped into the trunk

and, with a bright flash of light, they faded and disappeared.

Seconds later they reappeared in an abandoned gazebo in the jungle, precisely the place they had disappeared from only days before. In front of them, lying on the floor, were four empty buckets, just as they had left them. They picked up the buckets and made their way to a bubbling creek.

Captain Gunner, looking very smart in his black frockcoat and tricorn hat, approached them. "Hurry up!" he yelled. "You two are slacking off. Mahoot has made four trips while you've been lazing around. We're nearly ready to set sail for Cannibal Island."

Al and Jack smiled at each other. No one had missed them. "Sorry, Captain Gunner," said Al, "but we just had to say goodbye to Hally. She's happy not to be coming with us this time."

A boy about Al and Jack's age appeared along the track, carrying two full buckets of water. "Hello, you two." He smiled.

"Sorry, Mahoot, we got sidetracked," said Jack, "but we're back on duty now."

"These buckets are heavy," replied Mahoot. "I'll keep going and see you on *The Booty*."

"If young Hally's not coming with us you'd better get those barrels filled with water," Captain Gunner said. "The tide's in at four this afternoon, and we don't want to miss it." He turned and marched off down the track towards his ship.

"We did it!" whispered Jack, as he bent over the creek and filled his buckets. "We're getting better and better at coming and going from the Dragon Blood Islands."

The boys carried their buckets down the track to *The Booty*'s lifeboat, trying not to spill too much on the way.

"Lazy blighters," said Slicer, the cook, as Al and Jack emptied their buckets into the barrel set in the lifeboat. He turned to

Mahoot. "You've filled two barrels and worked hard so *you* can go back to *The Booty*." Slicer looked long and hard at Al and Jack. "You two have been slow and lazy, so you'll do double duty till the rest of the barrels are filled."

"Let's get it over with," said Al as he turned and trudged back up the track to the creek. "It will be worth all the hard work if we find the treasure on that map from Alleric Castle."

Sneaking Past the Jolly Roger

In the dead of night, with a following breeze, Captain Gunner stood on the poop deck of *The Booty*. "There are only two places that give safe anchorage on Cannibal Island," he explained to Al, Jack and Mahoot, as they studied the treasure map. "This map shows the second anchorage. Annoyingly, it's further around, past Blacktooth's fort, which means we'll have to sail right past the blasted thing.

To top it off, the landing beach is right near the cannibals' camp."

"Can we approach from another direction, rather than go near Blacktooth?" asked Al. "No," replied the captain. "There's a reef that runs along the island and Blacktooth guards the only entrance. We're gunner have to try to sneak past him. Mozzy!" he called to his bosun standing at the helm. "I want you to hoist the black sails. I don't want any reflection from the moonlight." Captain Gunner lifted his voice so it boomed across the ship. "I want total silence from here on or I'm gunner kill the first man who even sneezes!"

"Aye, aye," the crew responded.

With black sails billowing, *The Booty* had to make a tack under the walls of a large wooden fort. At anchor, just in front of the fort, was Blacktooth's ship, *The Revenge*.

"They're home, unfortunately," whispered Mahoot, as he and the rest of the crew peered intently at the forbidding walls nearby.

On a large lookout tower, the Jolly Roger, the black flag with the white grinning skull and crossbones, fluttered. The skull glowed in the moonlight. Slicer clutched his sword nervously as *The Booty* almost touched the shore below the fort. The bosun tightened a loose halyard so it didn't rattle against the mast in the breeze.

The Booty slid silently past and the fort disappeared behind them. Mahoot let out a huge sigh of relief. "Made it," he said under his breath.

They sailed on with a rocky reef on one side and a white chalk cliff on the shore. Pounding waves crashed over the reef and a huge rip tide dragged the ship sideways. With the surging currents and the white foam making the entrance extremely treacherous, only Captain Gunner's seamanship saved them from being shipwrecked. The pirates cheered once they were through and on their way to begin their treasure hunt.